WHEN KARMA MET FATE

WHEN KARMA MET FATE

GR THOMAS

G.R. Thomas

When Karma Met Fate

G.R. Thomas

Cover and Interior Design-GR Thomas

www.grthomasbooks.com

Content Alert

This is a story of fantasy fiction that contains sexual activity, fantasy violence, spousal abuse, and death involving blood and gore. There is talk of the death of a child and the depiction of traumatic childbirth.

Please read at your discretion.

Books by G.R. Thomas

The A'vean Chronicles—in reading order
Awaken (1)
Surrender (2)
Allegiance (3)
Redemption (4)
The First Satan (5)

Child of Fear and Fire
The Frangitelli Mirror

Symador Anthology

Dearest Chris,
It's all possible because of you.
You are my Karma and my Fate.
Eternally yours

"I pray you, do not fall in love with me, for I am falser than vows made with wine."

As you Like It – Act 3, Scene 5
William Shakespeare

When Karma Met Fate

Karma (Hinduism and Buddhism)

The sum of a person's actions in this and previous states of existence viewed as deciding their fate in future existences.

Fate (Greek and Roman Mythology)

Three goddesses who presided over the birth and life of humans. Each person's destiny was thought of as a thread spun, measured and cut by the three Fates: Clotho, Lachesis, and Atropo.

The development of events outside of a person's control regarded as pre-determined by a supernatural power.

Nothing existed forever.
Nothing was silent and dark...
until there was something...

I

In the beginning there was emptiness.
Cold, dark, and lonely nothingness.

The Nothing evolved. A syrupy primordial ooze stretched in patient silence towards a boundless darkness dotted with the brilliance of countless stars. The Nothing was underpinned by a never-ending universe.

Within this vacuous cold, consciousness first wrapped itself around Karma. A soft echo whispered her name. It urged her gently until she unravelled from infinity and opened her sight to a world of starlight. She blinked, the glare astounding, indescribable; and for the longest age, she stared at the boundless universe in silent awe.

That gentle whisper that nudged her into reality grew in pitch. It fanned her evolution, awoke the substance of her being, and coaxed her to explore the unknown laid out before her. The song of her soul joined in, and both coalesced in harmony. The refrain drew Karma from within herself until her very own tune strummed a rhythmic melody throughout the universe.

The music of creation tempted Karma from the thickness of forever, and promised a reprieve from her solitude. She reached forwards and spun endlessly, barrelling towards the strange and beautiful stars. They also whispered to her, just like that first, primal murmur. They called for her attention, yearning to know her just as she, too, sought the knowledge of who and what she was with them.

Karma swam towards the thickest smudge of stars. She fell into their heat, enraptured by their story, enamoured with their own birth... saddened with those that had died away. Even amongst those older than time, she knew no more of herself, so Karma floated away and cooled down on their dark side in a sea of ice and cloud. The music inside her strengthened, and she sang along to its hum. Her breath fanned the clouds away in tufts as her voice petered away into the nothingness.

Despite the joy of the song of the universe, Karma did not settle. The gentle cocoon of star cloud lost its comfort. The urge to know, to understand everything stirred an emptiness that grew within her. Something deep inside her tightened, an uncomfortable, insistent pressure. It urged her to keep moving, to search on, for what, she did not know. She found no place to feel contented, nowhere that fulfilled a tapping need within her, nothing to uncoil that burgeoning, lonely discomfort. Karma felt herself absorbed by the in-between, entranced by what lay beyond the stars. The unknown blackness between their shimmer was all too enticing. She slipped from the clouds and let herself fall towards it.

After a time, as Karma delved deeper into the reach of starlight, she lost the comfort of the voice that first called her name. Despite her own calls, it no longer whispered to her. The lack of its gentle murmur deepened her loneliness. Her insides felt like they might burst. The never-ending universe seemed to hold on tighter. She tugged and pulled from it and sped even further and deeper into the darkness, searching for comfort, for that unknown something.

As the star clouds that once warmed her faded into a faint smear, the strumming of the universe ceased. Karma stopped suddenly, the quiet of it like hitting an invisible barrier.

"I'm here, I'm here? Where are you?" she cried. There was no answer.

No more whispers, no more murmurings. No more did her name echo upon the ether. Even the stars refrained. Their gentle chatter was a memory.

"Please? Please don't abandon me?" Karma's voice cracked.

Silence pressed in on her. The dark in between the stars was no longer a glorious adventure. She screamed for her stars, called for their comfort, but they did not answer. Karma felt heavy, her dance amongst the universe now laboured, and the last threads of joy within her extinguished. She stopped, let the pull of the galaxies take control, and floated limply away into a cold and stark silence.

2

The gentleness of Karma stretched taught as loneliness overwhelmed her. She coasted through darkness; it felt thicker, her movements more difficult. Confusion took over as she wondered why the stars had abandoned her, why she had ever been created at all, and her soul shuddered.

Karma floated on until she found herself wrapped within in the pink and brown dust of a birthing star. It wasn't a voice, but it was something within the nothingness. The tingle of it against her form coaxed joy from its corner. Strengthened in the glory of it, she laughed and cried as the star blazed to life.

Smiling at the rhythm of its self-awareness, Karma looked out to the darkness.

"Hello? Are you there?" she called to the long quiet stars.

"I am here, with your young one," Karma called louder. Yet, the stars did not address her; they mumbled busily amongst themselves, a high-pitched indecipherable chatter. Despite their ignorance, Karma tarried on their outskirts, daring not to fall back away into the silent blackness, hoping for something, for anything. These blazing orbs felt like companions, even though she remained an outsider. Proximity to their joy dulled the edge of loneliness, as they too sought to find their own rhythm within the universe. Karma hooked herself onto this, and there she stayed.

Settled in the warmth of this celestial nursery for a time, Karma took comfort in the birth of new things, things that were raw and unsure, just like she was. She reached towards their infinite numbers, sang to them as though they were her very own. Their light was dazzling. It slipped between her limbs, consoling, alleviating, as if they now knew the meaning of everything, as if they had a story to tell... and she listened. Karma yearned for her own story, a destiny yet to be understood. She still had no genuine sense of self, of what exactly she was, of the purpose of her existence. When the company of the stars lost their comfort, when that tight ball within her overcame her once more, Karma retreated, feeling somehow unworthy of their light, and she flung herself back into the pull of space.

3

An invisible force tugged at Karma, hungry for control of her. It warped her shape this way and that. It pushed and pulled her with no mercy. She may have cried out, her tears crystalline droplets, her own song a melancholy scream as her form distorted. Her cries, unheard, petered away into the vast nothingness. In one moment, that force compressed her into a tiny speck of dust, and in the next, she screamed. Her voice rippled through the deep void as the nameless force stretched her a million miles wide, like a string of light... and it hurt. Karma yielded to it, giving in to that which she did not understand, to that which she could not control, and she melted into the quiet nothingness that engulfed her.

The pain did not ease, her cries were unbearable, and the fear so utterly consuming that Karma eventually resisted. She pulled away, tried to wrench herself free of the unseen entity that ruled over her, that invisible hand that demanded where she went and how she behaved. It gripped her tighter, pulled her mercilessly and flung her towards the hunger of a planet.

For a million years, Karma orbited a gaseous ball, a silent, vigilant jailor. She cried to no one, trapped within the sting of its wild storms, alone and terrified. She reached out every so often, feeling for something to grasp onto, searching for an escape, but there was nothing and no one to help. During that time, she obsessed with her purpose, her point of being, yet it all remained a mystery to her. So, exhausted, Karma curled back up, closed herself off, and slept for an eternity.

A meteorite shower awoke Karma. Icy debris plunged through her and the pain returned anew. The burning prickle unwound her, and her cry echoed, hollow and alone. Agony set alight her senses; she cried out again as her body moved. Clawing backwards, away from the grip of the planet, slipping away from the hottest length of the meteor, Karma called for that whisper, the gentle murmuring that had first awoken her into being. Silence deafened her, and she called with more earnest. She listened for the stars; they too did not respond.

The blackness between the light seemed even more unwelcoming, the depths of space darker than before. Karma curled in tight, her form trembled; iridescent speckles dusted from her. A fire as painful as the meteorite built within her, a strange pressure so different from the comfort and calm she once felt. Karma endured this unfamiliar sensation until it was too much, too strong... then she exploded, a white light expanding within the fire of the meteorite.

Silvery matter burst forth from her, like she was a birthing star, a new light within the darkness. Rage screamed from somewhere hidden deep inside her, and that anger made her grow... her life force strengthened, and Karma understood everything more than she did before.

When anger passed, and the pain of abandonment settled, Karma yawned and stretched in relief. What had hurt now tingled, what ached now pulsed warm and rhythmically. Her body moved freely... pleasantly. Karma gave into this new and exciting feeling. She savoured the rush through her form, every cell of her alive. She reached for herself, touched this part, caressed every curve, explored each crevice, groaning with the pleasure of the new sensations coursing through her soul. Karma screamed as ecstasy lit within her. Radiance billowed forth, the darkness obliterated, its greed for her soul retreating.

The song of Karma's pleasure dissipated away into the vastness until it faded into nothing, sucked up by an unending forever. Satiated, she continued along within the wake of the meteor's tail, still entrapped in its grip, but somehow contented.

Karma catapulted at a blinding speed. The stars stretched long and thin until the world about her blurred into whiteness, the air crisp and cool against her. The flaming rock dragged her across galaxies, both large and small; through boiling supernova clouds, thick and sticky with the entropy of what once was. She orbited the icy rings of a grey planet, buffeted wildly by its icy shards. Hooked by its gentler gravity, Karma found her chance. She reached out and wrapped herself around one of those icy spheres. Her form trembled, she wavered, and felt like she might explode once more. Yet, the ice settled the heat within her; she melded into its cold and escaped the meteorite.

She sat a while and rested herself in the outermost ring where the debris was small, a mere tickle that massaged her fresh pains away. There she stayed, recovering from the ache and shock of the journey, contemplating the strange new sensations she had discovered. It was within this moment of calm that an unknown voice echoed somewhere beyond.

Karma stared out into the pin-pricked darkness.

"Hello? Who is it?" Her form dusted the darkness with light as she called in earnest.

"Please? I am here. I am alone," she sang to the voice, her melody echoing away into the nothingness as she circled the cool planet. The unknown voice seemed to die away until silence once more pressed in. Karma's joy hollowed; her glow dulled. Pleasure ebbed away and loneliness wrapped itself around her once more.

Cold, near frozen, Karma existed in solitude for such an eternity that she felt she might fade away. Once more a shadow of herself, melting into the vacuous darkness from which she was born, the yawning void that existed before everything swallowed her. She wondered if, perhaps, oblivion might be preferable to the vastness of the unending lonely unknown that lay before her.

As time did not exist, Karma could not say when she first felt an unknown force tug at her. A new and tangible energy. She reached out and hooked onto it, catching hold of another great rock when it raced by, determined not to lose the scent of this birthing sound. She caught upon the fire of the comet's tail; its power more impressive than the last. It raced her away through a deep and utter blackness, the comet the only light heading towards a sound that seem to strum through her very essence. A new song, no, a thousand songs, and they seemed to call for her. A million intentions, questions and apologies floated about her, and she wanted to hear them, to listen, to soothe and comfort their sadness and woe. That tight coil within her unwound, her body released.

For the first time in her existence, Karma felt something akin to purpose, a quest, an intention to seek and to reprieve that which she herself had suffered. Those distant voices cried louder, brimming with a deep hollowness needing to be filled, a yearning to find purpose and comfort as well. Karma clawed along the comet's tail, growing, strengthening with the joy of finding something that beheld thoughts and feelings... something like herself, something alive.

The comet's energy was hot and comforting, a release from the clawing cold that had encapsulated her in ignorant safety. It roared through space, burning its way closer and closer, that sound more luscious, Karma hungrier for it by the moment. Her form tingled and shivered in that same pleasant way it had done when she had caressed herself, when she had cried out with rapture at the discovery of her senses. The comet dragged her past a trillion stars, old and new, beyond moons of ice and fire. She stretched and warped as they careened around a planet of roiling lava that spat her out into a new void speckled with a great white smudge... a brand new galaxy that held that song, that irresistible tune... a comforting rhythm that cupped her heart and enraptured her attention.

Karma found her voice and crooned back with earnest.

"I hear you!" she sang to this new rhythm. It reverberated in response, the sound already familiar, and Karma cried out louder, her melody sucked into the vastness of eternity, and it felt like bliss to not feel alone.

4

Karma held onto joy. Her song a continuous undercurrent of space. She grew, she strengthened further, as she revelled in the reward for her patience and her suffering. She promised herself that once she found the place that sung such love to her, that she would seek to do what this journey had done; bring light into darkness and release angst where pain and sorrow reigned. For those who suffered unjustly as she had, she would seek a reprieve.

By the time Karma tasted the pulse of this new world, her form had absorbed enough ice and dust, heat and light, that she had become visible. Her body filled out, its casing more sensitive, the surrounding space wrapped around her with luscious intensity. The touch of each star, the caress of a passing asteroid, filled her with bliss.

Light fanned from Karma's shape, a halo of who she was, a beacon calling for companionship. The cold, the heat, the prickling of matter rushing past seemed to rebirth her into something altogether new. Where once she was nothing but a thought, a formless, lonely presence, Karma now felt as strong and as substantial as the comets and meteorites that had plummeted her through space and time.

She marvelled at the design of herself, of the luminescence that streamed from each movement. Karma encompassed everything and nothing, stretching long and thin, then snapping back into a comforting orb before extending lithe limbs that could pluck at fine stardust. The song of the universe grew, it shaped and moulded her. Together, they evolved.

For centuries Karma floated along, listening, feeling, wondering on the source of the song that drew her on, bobbing through the galaxy, growing and perfecting. As she rounded a great burning sun, it plucked her from the orbit she floated upon and flung her closer to the new, murmuring world, the world that sung an irresistible melody.

Karma travelled on until she felt enveloped by its tune, until she could taste the love within it. She realised she had submitted to all that felt good and comforting, and that was her purpose, to reflect these feelings back. Sensation immersed her into a state of bliss as the coldness of space tingled and plucked at her being. Each rush, every prickle along her form, awoke something within her. A need for touch, a desire for comfort, a yearning for companionship.

Karma listened more intensely to the pulse of that mysterious world. Underpinning it, though, was something new, another rhythm, another consciousness, something entirely different from the song she sought. Her soul fluttered; her own pulse quickened.

"Hello?" she called to this new song. Its rhythm stuttered, and Karma knew it had heard her. She could taste something more than the fizz of the stars, and her life force raced a little faster. She thought her energy might explode from the joy as she meandered past barren, quiet worlds that held the faint echo of life extinguished. However, she tempered her joy as something echoed in the furthest reaches of her mind. She slowed down and folded in a little. That whisper urged caution, told her to quiet her desires, to put vigilance first, lest she tumble back into an existence of pain. Karma dulled herself, made her presence disappear... just in case.

As she rounded a grey moon, Karma hurtled towards a blue and green planet lit bright under its watch. The song that had wooed her was at its clearest... *this* was the place; *this* was where she was meant to be. She floated just above the pull of the planet and drank its melody in.

Tarrying for a time above the young planet, Karma hid within the blue glow of its moon before she circled alongside, learning its rhythm as it waltzed with the brilliant sun. She studied the world for an age, watched the movement of green across blue, saw it boil and cool, then erupt wildly, before it once more settled into calmness.

Existing for eons in the cool grasp of its upper atmosphere, Karma balanced upon the hunger of its pull, watching, learning, waiting to realise her purpose upon it. Her sensations blazed; her form billowed large, then small, then infinitesimal where she came to know the smallest particles that drove this wild new world. It tasted like a million things, smelled like heat and cold, life and death. She absorbed the energy emanating from far below. It was both beautiful and repulsive; it was joy and loathing. The universe held her in its grasp, but this world entranced her, bewitching her for another age.

Clouds massed and faded beneath her feet. When the

atmosphere rumbled with an unspent storm, it was dark and its lightning stung. When it was calm, it cocooned her, drifted along with her like a great cape. As the planet matured, its tumultuous activity subsided, its pace slowed, and its melody became a repetitive cooing that drew her focus to the blossoming of life... and this life expressed a repetition of chaos, love, hate, and ultimately, death.

It was in the mists of this planet that Karma's life force took a corporeal form for the first time. Where once her existence was pure energy, there was now something more tangible, something altogether new and real that could reach out and touch the world around her, and make a difference. The iridescent length of an arm entranced her. She curled the five strange digits on its end, enjoying the way they pressed together. Karma opened her mouth, sucked in the mineral tang of the atmosphere, felt it absorb deep within her, and she blew out a breath. A storm raged across the Earth from her power.

As she was marvelling at this metamorphosis, as Karma revelled in this emerging strength, she did not notice the threat hurtling in from behind her. The collision with Earth of a great icy comet blew her backwards. The deafening silence of space roared with the world's scream. Karma spun over and over, beyond the shimmer of the moon until she righted herself in the inky darkness beyond it. The explosion stunned her into submission. As she watched her dear world go quiet under the rage of the comet's impact, an icy tear slipped down her face. The world below, her world, choked on fire and smoke.

Karma floated a little closer, pressed her hands to her face, and cried harder. The world that spoke so sweetly to her was dying. Its oceans churned, they rose as tall as mountains and flooded the land. The landscape erupted and disgorged its fiery entrails across Earth, and the atmosphere clogged with a thickness that choked Karma as well. She eased away, tears filled her newly birthed eyes, and she cried a flood, trying to cool the fire of Earth. The rot of death, the sharp tang of burning flesh, filled each breath as ash rained across her world. Her tears streamed faster, to no avail, so she curled back up within herself and drifted back into sleep.

When awareness returned to Karma, she cried with joy, for she had thought her world destroyed, but once more it spun to its own new tune. She circled it, inspected each section to find it bedecked with an unfamiliar face, a new, more mature countenance. Expanses of white capped its head and its tail. The surface now draped in very different shapes of green and blue, their peaks and troughs like a distant cousin to the world she first discovered. Spots of smoke smothered large parts of some of the land, a fierce heat emanating into space that bit angrily against her. She breathed it in, hot and gritty, its taste so very different.

Floating to the edge of Earth's clutches, Karma frowned as she inspected her charge more closely. She held her breath and listened. Winds churned wildly, screaming noisily across the oceans. This world of hers sung a softer, more delicate song, the call of something new, something wild and in great need.

She drew in a breath and blew it back out. Sparkling cloud misted across Earth, cooling the residual heat of the collision and blowing the last of the debris away. Sunlight broke through the haze and drenched the sky. It bathed hungry lands below. Karma heard the spark of new life, the pushing of grass through dirt, the sweet smell of flowers bloomed, and the cry of an infant born. The atmosphere pulsed with the rhythm of life once more and Karma swelled with pride for restoring that which deserved to live.

Emboldened, Karma slipped deeper within the bounds of Earth. She breathed in the richness of it, a freshness that seemed to awaken something within her.... and she relinquished to the grip of it. Swept up in its cool winds, her skin tingled as rain drenched her body, her laughter peeled across the skies like thunder. Karma dove into a bilious storm cloud, reached out and slid along a lightning bolt until she found herself just a breath above a churning, grey ocean. Mountainous landscapes brimmed its horizon, jagged and tooth-like, and capped in ice.

Winds curled up from the waves below and pushed against Karma's body. It was richer with unfamiliar smells. It carried sounds of life that made her body shiver with joy, for she now knew that she was life, that she would sustain life, that she would join the world below and never feel alone again.

5

Karma prodded at her ever-changing form. It remained solid and tender, hot and cold, rippling with pain and pleasure... life lapped beneath the flesh that cocooned her. Where once her existence was no more than a thought floating through time, she felt plump and substantial; she felt real. Karma revelled in every atom that crashed against her. Flesh sang in response as her hands slid across every rise and fall of her body, as her fingers explored every part of her form. The wind was her song as she rejoiced at this new existence.

Karma marvelled at how she could coalesce into many tangible forms. One moment she existed as still as a rock, unmoving, the cold of the ocean pounding against her. Her form carved into sand and cliffs, leaving the salt of it crisp and lingering, and she thanked the ocean.

Upon the next storm, she pulled from the coastline and dissipated into a wispy cloud. Careening across blue skies, Karma braved blackened and green skies, endured skies that burned under the sun, and those that were frost filled at the very top of the world. She skimmed across deserts, sun-drenched her skin, hot air burning with each draw of breath. She balled tight as she swept along desert storms. The bite of the sand made her scream, her voice became the song of thunder. Wild, sandy winds lifted her up where the sun burned hottest, then plunged her back out across an ocean towards colder planes of green and brown.

Days, years, millennia rushed by as Karma devoured everything she could about Earth. Patrolling the great globe that she had watched burn and flood, and then rise again, she wanted to know everything about it, understand its pulse, feel its hurts and joys... be one with it.

Circling the planet through its darkness and its light, she plunged through all of its winters, heavy and crusted with frost. Her laugher was the snow that fell from her breath as she ran her fingers along the tallest snow-capped mountains. She slid along a glacier and spun back into the dry heat of its summers, cresting the hills of every continent, skimming the fine grass of each valley. Vast land masses offered their flavour and ignited senses long dormant deep within her.

The more she discovered of this wild burgeoning world, the stronger she felt, the more in control of her form she was, and it was that enticing beat of life strumming through the atmosphere that drew her to accept the Earth as her home... that and an intense, hollow loneliness she was now ready to overcome.

When Karma emerged from her adventure, an understanding fell upon her, a deep and confident knowing of her purpose. She looked up to a velvety sky, smiled at the blinking stars she once knew.

"I know who I am now." She would no longer feel lost

amongst them. Loneliness had once overwhelmed her, but now it had a rival, and it could no longer be ignored. With a symphony of need upon this planet, she would no longer let emptiness encapsulate her heart.

Karma skimmed the sky. Hovering in the security of clouds, wet with their touch, she stared into the fading darkness whence she came, setting it to memory, for that is what she felt it would remain. The voice that had first whispered her name remained silent when she called to it. She asked if her choice was the right one, if she was right to take this world to be her own. No one responded. The depths of the universe did not mourn her absence, and the loneliness that had invaded her very soul tapped at her to leave it all behind forever.

Karma turned away from her stars for the last time, said her goodbyes to whomever had given her life, and promised that no more would she dwell in dark abandonment. She did not miss the taste of nothingness, or the caress of a cold and lonely eternity. She knew she would never go back. Not even if they screamed and begged her, for she could not forgive the abandonment she felt.

Descending below the clouds, Karma stared anew at the green and blue and brown below. She closed her eyes and listened to the comforting rhythm of life within her reach. A warmth curled deep within her. It raced through her form and her eyes shot open. Love...she felt love for this world. Earth was her home, and she would guard it with her life.

6

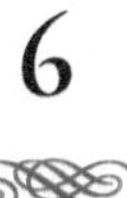

At first, Karma hid in the shadows, blended into shards of sunlight, squeezing herself between the hustle and bustle of the world whilst watching the two-legged creatures whose form she had replicated. They were strange, beautiful, complicated and brutal, and she had an overwhelming urge to protect them. Yet, she tread most carefully, yet to understand them at all. Their motivations, their purpose... it all remained a mystery, so she watched them in all their forms, in all their colours, for a thousand rotations around the brilliant sun.

At that tender moment when dawn and dusk meet across the middle of the Earth, when all was still for just a heartbeat, Karma listened to their yearnings, their joy and their torment. Her form rippled at the tiniest sound, the smallest cry for help, the mourning ululations of the lost and the dead. Desperate appeals for mercy to a hundred different deities pulled at the chords of her soul. Karma often looked back to the heavens when the moon was at its highest, deep within silken darkness, and she wondered of her creator, "Is it you they seek?"

Her creator remained forever silent. So too were they indifferent to the Earth-dwellers who sought the solace of a deity. Despite everything, despite her anger, after all the time passed, Karma had hoped her creator might answer, that they might indulge her query, and relieve the pains of these beings. Silence once more was the answer that solidified her resolve to never go back.

Her heart lurched for the disappointment the creatures of the Earth must feel. They did everything in the name of their deities, they worshipped, they fought...they even killed in their name. Humanity's cry was a desperate chorus that filled the quiet of her mind. It set her energy alight and she could no longer resist. She would no longer stand a passive witness. Her decision was instant. She would step in, she would right that which was wrong, and seek justice for the good and the innocent.

Karma could not resist the urge to help these weak creatures, to appease good deeds and sanction those most wicked. Something instinctual set her across the hemispheres in search of pain, seeking desperation and melancholy to resolve. She kept pace with the wind, learning its patterns. After a while, she took control of it and set its course. Sailing upon its breath, she coasted along its peaks and troughs towards the loudest cries of terror. The world roared; its pains so deep. Too many voices, too many screams, too many wishes bombarded her for reprieve.

Karma pulled to a stop, exhausted. The wind gusted wildly about her; it buffeted her form, polishing her skin until she shimmered like a star.

"One at a time," she whispered to herself. Karma was

one, they were many, and for now, she would start with one desperate soul.

Eyes closed, Karma honed in; her life force pulsed with a strange excitement as she singled out a mournful cry. Salty fear lingered on her tongue, her chest constricted, her breaths burned, and her body shivered in unison with the afflicted soul. Karma whispered to the wind. It scooped her up and plunged her down.

A wide, lush landscape opened up below as Karma shot across the sky, emerging into the embrace of a tepid, apricot dawn on the opposite side of the world. Leaves fluttered from the grip of their branches as she rushed below a treelined estuary that widened into a gushing river.

Creatures were abundant, dashing away, and taking flight as Karma scoured the water. She tilted her head, listening intently, running her fingers along its mirrored surface. She searched the shoreline, smelled fear, felt the desperate beat of a heart hasten by the moment. Karma brought the water to her lips and tasted the tremor of that heartbeat upon her tongue. It drew her towards a thick clutch of reeds swaying gently in the breeze. The *sh, sh,* sound of their movement tempered the cries she was following. Hovering above the river, she held her breath and listened intently.

Her face blossomed with a smile. "Ah, there you are."

The ammonia tang of human fear plunged sharply into her next breath, and she followed the odour. Slipping beneath the cool river water, her feet sunk into a soft bed of sand. She moved slowly, meticulously. The tremor of human flesh rippled through the water, lapping against her skin when she parted a woody curtain of reeds.

Karma came upon a sun-touched man, a withered human of an age not long for this world. He cowered within the thickest, deepest part of the reed bed. The reeds whispered under the tremble of his terror, giving away his place of hiding from whatever terrified him. Of course, he could not see her. His wide, red-rimmed eyes stared straight through her.

Knobbed hands pressed over his mouth as he struggled to hold his breath, to quell the sound of his terror. Thick, dirt-laden tears breached his greying lashes. They slid down his face, mixing with strings of drool hanging from his chin. His terror was so palpable that Karma knew without a doubt her sudden appearance would be too much for him to bear. His life force was already weak, the beat of it irregular and fluttering, even his scant breaths rattled, the pink of his lips already a shade too dark. So, Karma remained on a different spectrum, shadowed within the cracks of visible light, lest she bring upon him an untimely demise.

The human reached awkwardly for purchase along the shoreline. He slipped along its slimy lip. His fear birthed into a loud scream, and he slapped over his mouth once more with a trembling palm, barely stifling those ragged breaths. Drool beaded heavier along his jawline, peeling away down into the river that sucked hungrily at his waist. He clambered repeatedly up the reeds, his palms bloody from clawing armfuls of shredded foliage. His weight and weariness dragged him back down, and he slipped deeper into the water. Flies buzzed around him, tapping at the moisture pooling in his eyes. He cried out again; the sound tore at something within Karma and she followed the direction of his bulging eyes.

The stillness of the water broke as a ripple formed just

below its surface and gained speed as it approached the reeds. Bubbles popped silently; the ripples closer by the moment. The man's struggles intensified, the water about his waste yellowed. Karma slipped beneath the surface. Curiosity and concern dilated her eyes as she searched the current.

The water quickly became murky as she sunk lower, wading towards the centre of the river. The current churned harder, tossing her left, her toes curled, gripping into the sand bed. Karma released a little light to see her way through the darkness. The silty blend of the water quickly gave way to a slow-moving shadow. She could feel the steady poise of its energy, the patient, calculated drive of its movements. Her essence fanned brighter, lighting the water about her a little more.

Karma pulled back, aghast, as a great toothed beast slunk towards the shallows. Clawed feet paddled towards the reeds, oily eyes searched with no hint of emotion. Karma felt the rumble of its belly and tasted its hunger. The creature camouflaged within the roots and debris below the waterline, its growl floated across the current. Its eyes blinked slowly; its jaw slackened to half open. A pasty tongue rimmed with razored teeth caught in her light. Karma fell away, dulled her fluorescence and rose from the water; urgency sped her choices. The cowering man did not feel her peer into his soul. He had no awareness of her filing through his past, through the good and the bad of his life. She probed his racing heart, searched it for darkness, for cunning and evil. All the while, he clambered pointlessly at the shore, his aged body giving out in the thick sludge dragging him back in.

Relief flooded Karma. His heart was pure, his deeds all done in good faith, a life well lived. She smiled at him, knowing he was unworthy of such a demise, especially when eternity was to call upon him so soon.

Karma looked back to the ripple of the water; it was so very close now. As frightening as this beast was, she also sensed its drive was not of predetermined evil. She frowned; this creature was also unworthy of being denied a meal, of suffering the pain of hunger. Hesitating for a moment, Karma pondered her choices as she placed herself between the two beings. The hunter moved through the world without malice, driven purely by emotionless, unbiased instinct. As it came within lunging range, Karma slipped back under the water and entered the meat and bones of the noble creature. She turned its mind to another meal grazing by the shoreline downwind. It rolled, flicked its tail, the old man forgotten. Karma withdrew from it and coiled her way back through the reeds to see the human cry in relief.

She sunk beneath the man's flesh, felt the exhaustion within him. Her energy gave movement to his weakened limbs. Karma drove his muscles to stretch and contract. Eventually, with her help, he pulled free of his plight. With each movement, there was a discovery of human senses that she revelled in. The way mud oozed through his fingers, the feel of sand beneath his feet... the coursing of his life force throughout his very being. Karma struggled to remove herself. His soul magnetised her, as she became enraptured by the way he experienced the world through touch and feel. The craving to *feel*, to touch, to know the world differently was almost too consuming, and for a moment, Karma lost herself within him.

A frantic voice drew Karma from her infatuation, and she

withdrew from the man. An elderly woman bustled their way. Karma felt momentarily unable to look at the woman, even though she knew the woman was wholly unaware of her presence. Heat flushed throughout Karma's soul for the intimacy she had shared exploring the man.

Karma pressed her hands against her face, felt the warmth emanate through her skin. The linger of sensation pressed against her, within her. Something shifted throughout her soul, a new and unrivalled connection with humanity, and she knew without a doubt that she would die for them.

As the old man caught his breath in the cool mud rimming the bank, the woman approached, limping quickly towards him, her body heavily pressed against a staff. Whispering papyrus tugged at her clothing, drew blood to her skin, but she did not heed the pain. Crying, her staff fell away, and she slid down beside the man, lips pressed to his forehead, arthritic fingers holding onto his as though to never let go.

Tears shone down Karma's face as she relinquished the plunder of sensation, a voice deep within her already yearning for it again. She slipped away, laced within the reeds, a gentle smile upon her lips as she watched the man being helped to safety, coughing and retching further in from the shore. The woman soothed him a while longer until he recovered enough to stand, and arm in arm, they wandered away, whispering their love to each other over and over.

Karma swelled with warmth, the fire within her stoked to a blaze, and she settled herself firmly upon the Earth.

7

Karma had not returned for a generation to the home of the old man she had saved. Yet, in all that time, the memory of him lingered, the recollection of what it felt like to feel what he felt, to smell and to taste, to fear and to be reprieved. Long gone was he, but many more followed, many who needed her attention, her intervention, and in many, Karma had partaken a taste of their worldly experience by merging with them as they slept.

It was in this way that she discovered Aka, and it was here that she roused on a new day. Morning sunlight struck Aka's face, setting a golden glow upon her skin and tempting her eyes to open. Karma slid from Aka's soul, unbound from her emotions before she awoke, satiated by her dreamscape and the strange turmoil her body crested throughout slumber.

Karma floated above Aka, smiled, wishing she could say thank you, but knowing to do so would strike a fear through Aka that Karma feared she might drop dead. Content to remain a shadow, a dream, Karma gave in to the call of the day.

The din of mundanity punctured her serenity the moment her connection with Aka was severed. The constant demands of her people pressed against Karma, tempting her to fold back in on herself, to rest as Aka did. Not a moment was silent. Not a second did the city cease braying with hope, with fear, with desperate pleas to ease, and to avenge... and Karma saw to it all.

This morning, she tarried, wafting like a wisp of cloud out of Aka's humble home. She set herself atop a golden pyramid, the largest of them all, the one that guarded the land. There Karma rested, watching her people, listening as dawn smudged from a bruise to an apricot, the burning disk of the sun casting deep shadows, and these shadows were not silent. They brimmed with the song of humanity, and another voice, one that she had heard so long ago, a voice with a beat like her own.

Karma squinted, tilted her head, stared long into the murky eye of the shadows. She breathed the crisp morning air and closed her eyes.

"Who are you?" Karma's breath misted, quickly dissipating under the heat of the sun. Of course, there was no answer. She expected this.

She refocused on the city, on the smell of roast meat, the call of street traders, and the ever-present need of her intervention. Karma had visited this thriving community many times since the beginning. She felt drawn to this community more than the north and the south, as it required an equal measure of her punishment and redemption. Its need was great.

But it was truly something else that held her there. Within this sand-strewn land, that unknown, yet familiar voice hooked onto the wind, its song ever-present but always unreachable. A voice that trilled above others, that lured her to stay, the one that so far had refused to answer her call. It whispered in shadows, slipped between cracks, the vibration of it so very familiar, yet Karma could not quite catch it.

Her shoulders slumped, she sighed and let her eyes glaze, still feeling for the rhythm of the voice... a palpable energy always left in its wake. Karma's skin shimmered as the song still weighed upon the air, its echo upon her every breath. Her fingers twitched, hand reaching out as though she might pluck that 'other' from the ether. Her fingers raked through nothingness and dropped by her side. Rising from the golden peak, her energy felt more sluggish, yet she embarked on another day of organizing the world.

This city, her city, already teamed with more life than Karma could cope with. Each day new infants drew their first breaths, and others their last. It was within the bounds of first and last breaths that Karma focused. Choosing who and where to intercede was becoming harder every day. It wasn't always the loudest cries that she answered, it was more often than not, the meekest, most humble of whispers that drew Karma to someone's side.

Tapping into the morning, she scouted for such calls through the bustle of a burgeoning day. Horse and donkey hooves clattered below her course, accompanying interesting and repugnant smells. Humans called about narrow, winding streets, some with joy and others in utter misery. This city congealed with everything good and abhorrent about the humans she loved.

At first she had watched the way these complicated beings behaved, not touching them the way she had that man so long ago. She studied their habits and rituals, their strange mannerisms, and the way they treated one another. There was a cadence to it all. At times it was satisfying, but more often than not, their rituals made her want to collapse like a star and disappear back into the nothingness of oblivion.

Something inexplicable drove humanity, and it all came down to one main thing that had taken her eons to understand... the tenderness of their flesh pressed against one another. That, married with a strangeness in their understanding of the universe, had hooked Karma. It had stoked her appetite to understand, to *feel* more.... and to know that alluring song that teased from the shadows.

8

Over time, Karma strengthened her resolve as she understood these people more intricately. Right and wrong were more complicated as time passed. The correct destiny was not always a straightforward choice. It was a matter of intricate balance that made Karma more decisive with her justice, never mulling over or second-guessing her decisions. She had learned to accept that she could not fulfil her duty as she truly wished, that not all could receive the deserved outcome of their actions. They bred incessantly and spread rapidly across the continents. The rise of the population meant more and more people escaped her justice, while others were denied the reprieve of her gentle hand.

Once, long lost to the fog of passing time, she had saved them all; Karma had believed in the essential goodness underneath ignorant behaviours. However, after the last great pyramid rose to guard over the endless sands, Karma's heart seemed to hollow as she witnessed thousands killed to be buried with their pharaoh. Loyal servants, women, children, even cats and alligators were slaughtered to follow a mortal...

to nowhere. It was no better in the northern and eastern lands. Humans possessed a capacity for immense harm through both ignorance and greed, and that irresistible need for the pleasure of flesh against flesh.

When the last stone sealed the greatest great king in his tomb, Karma's soul hardened a little more, and she had never looked upon humans with quite the same joyous abandon. She now understood humans were beyond complicated. There was no sense to so much that they did. They were far from the innocent souls she had fallen in love with so long ago.

Both endearing and horrific all at once, she spent another age in hiding, watching them to see if they could moderate their own justice, hoping with abandon that they might settle in a calmer, kinder rhythm. They could not, and she cried more deeply, her tears washing into the great river that divided their city. She filled its coffers until it breached its banks and the darkness flooded, washing away the evil. Karma whispered to the wind to bring forth such a flood each year to cleanse the corruption that rebuilt time and again.

Karma withdrew, burying herself deep within the cooler, northern most horizon where humanity was simpler, less advanced. She curled up and plunged into stasis for another millennium to contemplate what she should do.

9

When Karma emerged from her solitude, she had devised a strict protocol for justice and compassion. She unwound from her hiding place in a mountainous range of ice and snow and slipped back within the heat of the mid-eastern lands.

What she found displeased her, and she blew a great dust storm in from the desert. Circling her fingers, sand drew into a funnel and she blew again. Her storm spun across the river, burying the death monuments, extinguishing the ones who pandered to them, the ones who killed in the name of things which did not exist. Karma smiled with satisfaction; their leaders could not put any more innocents to death within the monumental stone structures. She called upon the clouds and washed the city clean, asked the sun to shine strong, and as the people emerged, they found their crops sprung, the herds fat and healthy. Karma waited to see if they had learned a lesson.

From dawn to dusk, Karma travelled the busy streets, crested less populace savannahs, and found more love than hate. She smiled, and when she smiled the wind blew gently, the sun shone less sharply, and humans had an easier time with their daily routines.

Despite her hard work, it was exhausting keeping up with human evolution. They were never content; they moved increasingly further from their homeland, mingling with different peoples. Sharing what they knew, they exchanged goods and ideology. It did, for a short while, seem a good and prosperous endeavour. Yet, as their knowledge expanded, their idolatry also grew, and they fell back into old patterns of both loving and loathing one another. Yet, Karma persisted because she loved them despite how cruel they could be.

The beauty of the way they loved drew her further from memories of the loneliness of eternity, memories of her dear long departed Aka kept a warmth bubbling behind her breast. Humans gave her something to look forward to with each turn around the brilliant sun. At the end of every day, when the moon relieved the heat of the day, it was love that drove her, and love Karma did.

10

Karma sunk below a smattering of clouds. She fell upon a gust beyond the city, heading towards her new beloved. The gentle curves of Aka's body, the softness of her skin, the way her teeth shone like pearls when she smiled... these memories of Aka kept that hollow place within Karma subdued. Aka had opened Karma up to the beauty of human love and it spurred her on, generation after generation, to seek it out.

Karma breathed deep, the cool of dawn always crisper, cleaner and easier to tap into. She tasted the air for fear, drank it in, filtered through the sourness of the desperate and the greedy. Closing her eyes, she searched for the perfume of passion. Her heart yearned for the sweetness of its syrupy warmth. An addiction that set in with Aka generations ago, Karma had rekindled that with Kehtut.

Drifting above a new palace that centred the city, Karma banked right above the baying of an over-worked donkey laden with heavy packs. She twisted through a spice market; already bustling, each breath rich and delicious, the walkways stained red and ochre with its spoils. She blended with the air and sifted through an early rush and crush of bodies, opening their businesses, none the wiser that Karma was present.

When the fragrance of the market place faded, the freshness of the river's edge rose to greet her. A gently lapping shoreline led her to the humbler side of the city. Her motion quickened; heat flushed through her. She looked up at the fading, new moon. It was only under its watch that she visited Kehtut, and it was only in these moments that Karma understood and worshipped the female form more. She melded with it, revelled in its gentle softness, her soul released for just a moment from the enormity of her existence. Karma could almost feel the curve of a breast under her touch. A gasp escaped her. Birds startled from a nearby tree and Karma giggled to herself, her laugh the buzz in the air when all else was quiet.

The foul stench of drying fish snapped Karma from her reverie. Strung out for days. Even she pressed a hand over her mouth, but it only pushed her quicker. It was pulling a drowning calf from the river that she first found Kehtut. Her day's catch lost, Kehtut had thrown her net out to hook the baying animal and drag it in. Karma had heard the rumble of Kehtut's stomach that night. She had felt hollow and starved along with her. Karma fell in love the night she watched Kehtut and her new husband, Anwar, feed the calf the last of their milk.

She smelled the spicy, musk essence of Kehtut before she saw her. A comforting warmth washed through Karma. Her form fluttered into visibility as she struggled to contain the urge within her.

Kehtut appeared in a doorway, a hand shielding her eyes

from the strike of the rising sun across the glass of the river. Karma hovered within smoke billowing from the hearth of the dwelling next door. Kehtut wandered to the river's edge, reached down and splashed water across her face. She stood, water beading down her bronzed skin. Kehtut peered left and right, her hand ghosting the empty mooring, Anwar not back from the early catch. Karma flickered again. She sunk deeper into the hearth smoke and studied the river for his return. Anwar taught Karma how to worship a woman, and for this reason, she loved him deeply as well.

Kehtut turned back, her hand circling a small swelling. Karma smiled anew. Her delight at the joy of a new life was short-lived, as she immediately feared for the future of this little being. Another soul to protect. The weight of her destiny thinned her down ever so slightly.

Kehtut turned back as a call came from the river. Karma followed the sound of water sloshing and wood clunk against wood. A thin boat moored and Anwar appeared, carrying a string of dripping fish over his back. He dropped his fishing rods and baskets by the boat. Wandering by a small yard, he reserved a pat for his old horse.

"Good girl, Zeahne, an extra treat for you today, my love." Anwar reached into a leather pouch dangling at his waist, his hand outstretched under the velvety muzzle. Zeahne immediately snatched up a plump date. The horse snorted through her treat, her head bobbing up and down as the date glued inside her palate. Anwar laughed. "You silly old thing."

Karma's essence fanned with love, for whomever should love an animal, she had learned, almost always had a soul most gentle.

Anwar set his fish to dry across a woven mat. He stretched out his limbs, cracked his knuckles, and yawned widely. Tall, muscled and darker than Kehtut, the undulations of his body, the midnight of Anwar's eyes, never failed to stir something within Karma. She knew in these moments that she was more alike with humans than she cared to think. Something universal connected them.

"Love!" Kehtut threw her arms around Anwar and their lips connected. The taste of cloves lingered on Karma's tongue from that kiss, and her form seemed to melt as she felt their skin press together. Yearning for the one thing existence denied her, *touch*, was what drove Karma to Kehtut and Anwar, and so many before them.

In every form available to her, Karma had tried to understand touch, to experience what the humans did, but it was only when she had discovered she could sink beneath their skin, to meld with a human for just a small time, that Karma became addicted to the sensuality of flesh on flesh. The tingle and heat of lovemaking fed her soul. It helped her forget the time before, the time of darkness, the endless eons of crushing solitude.

As Anwar released Kehtut's rich lips, Karma glided from within the smokestack, rolled down the side of the building and slid a little closer, staying hidden between fresh slices of sunshine. Anwar laced his fingers through Kehtut's. A knowing smile brightened his weary face and set a fresh sparkle in his eyes. Karma felt the vibration of his heart quicken and blood surge to his loins.

Kehtut reached towards an urn by the entry to their home. She dipped deep into it, red wine sloshed from a smooth wooden cup. She held it to Anwar's lips. Anwar smiled as he drank deeply, his throat bobbing with thirst. Anwar's tongue swept slowly across his lips. He sucked in the lower one, snagging it between his teeth. Kehtut mirrored him. She set the cup to her lips and drank. Kehtut ran her finger across her lower lip, wine coloured her skin. She slipped her finger into Anwar's mouth, and both their hearts pounded faster.

Karma tasted the wine. Her head seemed to spin; the air felt hotter than before. She edged closer as Kehtut dipped a cloth in another urn. She washed Anwar's hands, her movements deliberate, gentle. Their eyes hooked upon each other and Karma felt the cool of the water run down her own body. As she sighed, a breeze rushed from within her. It pressed at the couple. Anwar guided Kehtut back towards the privacy of their home, disappearing behind the flap of tanned hide that was the door.

Karma had to make her move quickly. She peered up, called upon the wind, and it listened to her plea. A sharp gust blew, it rustled the entrance to their hut and Karma rode along with it, slipping through a crack in the doorway. In the space of a breath, Karma melded into Kehtut, her possession masked by the touch of the breeze, the woman none the wiser that Karma quietly dwelled within the outskirts of her mind.

A small fire crackled inside the dwelling, the air rich with the smell of fat and wine. A meaty stew bubbled steadily atop a trivet; fresh bread cooled nearby. Kehtut unravelled a woven mat, smoothed a bull pelt across it, and kneeled in front of Anwar.

Anwar smiled; long lashes veiled his eyes in a suddenly coy expression. He looked down. His chest moved a little faster, his fingers pressed against his palms. His eyes flicked sharply back to Kehtut. She patted the mat between them.

With a curl of her finger, Kehtut had Anwar's knees buckle beneath him. Karma felt the rush of Kehtut's heart, the sensual prickling of her skin and the irresistible warmth blossom between Kehtut's thighs. She wanted to run her hands down the length of Kehtut's body, over the rise of her breasts and down.. down... down... but it was not for her to start such things. It was for them alone to guide their passion.

Anwar rested his hands around Kehtut's waist. He urged her to stand. Head leaning gently against the roundness of her belly, Anwar breathed in her scent. His next breath rumbled from his chest like the growl of a lion. Karma looked down upon him through Kehtut's eyes and she wished to smell what he smelled, to feel Kehtut the way he did. For now, though, she stayed where she was, her soul captured, enraptured, her breath held for what was to come.

The first kisses dusted across Kehtut's belly. Karma's soul moaned along with Kehtut. Anwar's hands slid the length of Kehtut's thighs, his fingers slid under her clothing and pushed her skirt up. He bunched the linen in his fists. A deeper groan rumbled in Anwar's throat. Kehtut responded with a gasp. Karma felt dizzy and hot. Kehtut pushed Anwar's head closer to the apex of her thighs. Her hands massaged his rich black hair, guiding his rhythm. Karma felt the fibres smooth through her fingers, and the restraint of Kehtut dragging the moment out.

Karma coiled deeper within Kehtut as Anwar's tongue made its way up her inner thigh, kissing here, licking there. Karma's mind exploded when his mouth sank between her legs. The rhythmic sweep of his tongue had Karma as jealous as she was euphoric. Kehtut's breaths quickened, her hands curled tighter through Anwar's hair. He moaned, pressed his tongue deeper, sweeping it in, then out. Kehtut cried out as heat flooded her. She clutched Anwar's head to steady the shudders raking through her body. Anwar hugged into her, feeling the pulse of her joy upon his tongue, breathing in the sweet smell of her pleasure. When Kehtut's bliss calmed, she slowly sank to the floor. Diamonds star-pricked the secret void Karma dwelt in. Ecstasy wrapped her in an addictive heat.

Karma moved with Kehtut as she eased Anwar onto his back. Karma closed her eyes as Kehtut sat astride Anwar, filling her body with him. She moved with a practiced rhythm, with a knowing of what made Anwar's eyes roll back. Anwar moaned; his skin glistened. His fingers pressed into Kehtut's buttocks, guiding her, ensuring all of him was within her. They rocked back and forth. Karma tasted his passion, the power of his love filled Kehtut until ultimately there was a cry and a release. Kehtut fell forwards over Anwar, their bodies slick and hot, their breaths slowly settling. They murmured gentle words to one another.

Karma rested a while as Kehtut lay wrapped in Anwar's powerful embrace. She floated on the pleasantness of their love whilst their bodies settled and their hearts calmed.

She slept as they slept, roused when they roused, the pressure of Anwar's body a tell that they were not yet done. This time, in the second before his eyes opened, Karma slipped from Kehtut into the peripheries of Anwar. It was from this perspective that Karma found the most joy. The feel of

Kehtut, the smell and the taste, the softness of her skin and curves of her body were so much more alluring.

Kehtut giggled as Anwar tickled her awake. Karma delighted in the way Kehtut's flesh shivered under his touch. Gentle, giving careful space to her belly, Karma cried with joy as Anwar lift her skirt once more, and plunged his tongue deep within Kehtut. Karma groaned as he groaned. The taste upon his tongue set a fire within Karma's soul. The soft folds of Kehtut sent Karma's vision to blackness, light peppering the darkness until Kehtut cried out again. As Karma's bliss mirrored Kehtut's, the wind gusted around the home, whistling and tapping at the roof.

Eyes hooded, they rolled under the bull pelt and drifted to sleep once more, Karma allowing herself the pleasure of rest; a brief reprieve from her burdens.

Releasing from that afterglow was always difficult. Karma clung to it for as long as she could, but let go she did, for she was merely a silent passenger in their lovemaking, and she knew when to let go, when to give them back their privacy.

Her small moment of ecstasy ended more quickly than usual on this day. Still drunk with the memory of touch, the flavour of Kehtut strong within her, annoyance rose within Karma when she sensed violence nearby. Normally, she would ease away in the depths of their dreams, but today she could not afford Anwar this courtesy. She had to disconnect quickly. The smell of rot and imminent death pierced through her contentment.

Karma peeled herself away in the space of a breath, floated momentarily over Anwar, who gasped awake from the horizon of sleep. He clutched his chest with fright as the connection severed. Karma blew sleep back towards Anwar and set the echo of a kiss on Kehtut's forehead. She yawned, rubbed her eyes and sunk back into the crook of Anwar's arm.

Almost instantly, the sensuality of Anwar and Kehtut faded. A cold emptiness slithered through Karma as she left the cosy home. Elevated above the roof under the stark glare of a mid-morning sun, she sucked in the world's smell. The mundanity of her existence washed the last of her pleasure away.

Staring intently across the city, Karma reached out for the anger that had disturbed her joy. The air wavered, its vibration sharp and unpleasant. She felt the violence of the target of her justice. The rage that coursed through him hit Karma well before she saw him. His energy was all too easy to track. A broad smile bloomed across her face. Today's justice would be well served, and that understanding had Karma speeding through a dozen tight alleys, careening sharply left at the city centre, where she stopped between a strike of sunlight and a shadow. There, she listened.

A guttural scream drew her attention behind the main temple, its large columnar entrance casting deep shadows over the hovels that hugged it for dear life. Karma slid around a corner, her eyes narrowed and her soul shook. Where the sun could not penetrate, in the stinking creases overlooked by most, somewhere lost in the recesses of life, a woman begged for mercy. Karma dropped, spun around and reformed into a gust. She slipped between walls, scooped under door cracks until she rose back up into the relief of the sun and crested a dilapidated hut. There she hovered... watching.

Karma's form shimmered, misted out of air into a thin

cloud, then strengthened into the faint outline of her human form. Her limbs were long, bioluminescent hair draped her head, glimmering along her length, covering the nakedness of her body. Karma's fingers clenched; each fist pulsed with light, brighter and brighter. Her energy simmered with the heat of impending justice. The screams intensified.

Karma's head snapped to the right of the small dwelling as a woman's body tumbled backwards through the flap of fabric that covered the doorway. Breath punched from the woman's chest. She gasped for air and curled up into a small, trembling ball.

Like the sun glancing across water, Karma's essence shimmered along the ground below. Heat built quickly within her. Not that delicious passion she felt with Kehtut, but the fiery burn of vengeance.

The woman unwound, fingers clawing for purchase, caked in dirt as she scrambled along the ground, away from the hovel. Coughing up blood, she rolled to her side, knees tucked up against her chest. Her breaths were jagged, yet she tried to shimmy like a snake away from the yelling and banging within the hovel.

Dried and glistening blood crusted her face. Her eyes were blackened, the deep umber of her skin lacked the vitality of health. Karma's soul tensed further; an angry coil ready to unleash.

Flies buzzed around the woman's face as she drew a breath and screamed. Her words cried for help. Terror split her lips; spittle foamed in the corners of her mouth as her cries weakened with each gasp of breath. No human came to her aid.

Karma extended her hand. She cast out a chord of light.

It coiled down and painlessly pushed itself into the woman's nostrils. Her light travelled within the woman, felt her energy, tasted her thoughts, recalled her memories. Karma puffed herself out, satisfied that goodness outweighed corruption. She pulled her light away. The woman gasped, looked up into the shadows and the single, blinding shard of sunlight that cleaved through it.

She mumbled for the God she worshipped.

"It is not He, dear one. It is I, Karma," Karma whispered into the woman's soul. The woman stopped her writhing for a moment and calmed her breathing. She pressed trembling fingers to her heart as though she felt Karma's soothing message.

A deep bellow jolted the woman from her fugue, and she resumed her desperate crawl to freedom. She screamed hoarsely, coughed, spat more blood. Her movements laboured as she heaved for breath and escape.

Content with her judgement, Karma rolled her hands together. She called upon her energy and sunk closer to the ground. Feet setting upon a hard-packed earth, Karma's form remained hidden in the shadows. She smirked as the perpetrator burst out of the home.

A knife glinted in that slice of sunshine. It reflected slivers of light across the courtyard, lit up the toothless maw of a short and stocky man. His mouth twisted into a sneer the moment his eyes narrowed upon the woman. Sweat beaded down his forehead, the salt of it stung and blurred his vision. He blinked, rubbed beady, emotionless eyes, baring rotten teeth as he yelled through the discomfort. When his eyes cleared and he found the woman again, his truth did not need to be probed. Karma could see through his eyes, and what she saw was unfiltered hatred.

"Whore, get back here! You will do as I say. I claim ownership of you. You *will* submit to me!" He sniffed and spat a wad of phlegm, waving the knife. Karma grimaced; her fingers curled repetitively; her outline opaquer by the moment.

Twice the size of the woman, violence twitched in his muscles. Karma drew her power to its fullest. A mirage; she shimmered just beyond his perception and absorbed the hot air around her. It rushed throughout her form, burning and fanning the fire of justice within her. It twisted with wrath; her hands were now fists. Her rage gusted against the man, enough that he swayed.

He stumbled, then leaned down; knobbed, filthy fingers fisted through the woman's plaited hair. He dragged her along the ground, the sound course as her skin sheared across the rubble. She kicked, she screamed, her voice cracking, failing. He flipped her over and straddled her. Drool streamed from his mouth. He laughed; the odour of ale so strong on his breath that Karma could smell it at a distance. Something reflected in the sun as he reached to his hip. He raised the blade above his head. Karma readied herself, fingers releasing, ready to strike him down.

A flash of light struck over Karma's shoulder. She flinched, her energy still coiled within her, unused. Spinning about, she searched for the source, turning quickly back as the lasts breaths of life purged like a horn from the man's throat. Karma's hand remained still, unwavering above her head, yet to strike.

She watched the man in awe as his body froze. The knife

slipped from his stunned fingers and made a high-pitched *ting* sound as it glanced from a rock, landing just beside the woman's wide-eyed expression. The man's eyes bulged; a trickle of blood pooled in the hollow of his throat; his mouth gaped for breath. The woman gasped, screamed and rolled away. Her body scraping further across the coarse ground, the taste fresh blood flooded Karma's next breath.

The man slumped and fell forward with a heavy thud, dust plumed about his head. The woman scrambled further away, pulling herself to her feet. She gasped, hugging her torso, eyes darting around, confused. Hand shielding her eyes, she peered upwards to where Karma hovered, unseeing of her. The woman wiped the blood from her mouth with trembling hands. She plucked sweat-laden braid from her face and smoothed it behind her ears. Her body relaxed a little as she pulled her torn clothing up, ensuring her breasts were covered. Karma felt the lump in her throat as the woman swallowed nervously, eyes thinner as she searched for the source of her tormentor's demise. As that fine slice of sun beat down on her face, the woman looked towards the sky and placed her hands together.

"Hathor... Hathor I thank you. I am your servant." Eyes closed, she muttered more silent words, bowed low to the ground and kissed it. Karma smiled to herself, pleased that the woman had solace in something, even though that something did not exist. The woman shifted; she pushed herself back to her feet and dusted herself as clean as she could; she straightened her back and squared her shoulders. Beads clinked around her neck as she smoothed her hair down her back. Her attention hooked on the body near her feet. Leaning over the man's corpse, the woman huffed.

"Pig!" She spat atop his head and screamed until the veins of her temples bulged. Karma drew her pain away, let it run through her own soul, smiling once more as the woman ran away, not once looking back.

After the vibration of the woman's footsteps faded, and the smell of her blood gave way to the thick stench of the city, Karma returned her attention to the immediate surroundings. She coasted across the alley, stepped over the husband's corpse and squinted towards each shadow, peered around each corner. There was nothing but dust and excrement with a smattering of whitened bones around the char of a firepit. She shut out the world, opened her inner eye, breathed deep and cut ties to the sounds of the physical world.

The gentle swell of a presence rippled the calm of the ether. The faintest of melodies probed for her attention. It plucked at her; a shiver ran through her innards.

"Hello?" Karma called. It was that voice she had heard long ago, the one that never returned her call, the one that felt a little like her.

Karma folded in a little, faded back to nothingness and clasped her hands to her chest as humans did when they, too, were nervous. She turned around once, twice, staying within the confines of a shadow a few feet from the now fly-ridden corpse. She shivered again, the air strangely cooled, despite the bite of summer heat. Karma stepped to the edge of the shadow, flies buzzing through her concealment, the stench of death stirred revulsion within her. She searched about for the cause of the colder air, listened for a melody. A stronger echo reverberated upon her next breath. A voice lay its way through her mind. She searched for the energy that felt just like her own, the energy that had dispatched the human man the way she had intended to do.

"Who's there?" Karma's voice wavered, quickly lost on a gust of wind. She coiled back and rose above the roof line where the air choked with smog. It kept her hidden as she squinted past a thousand chimneys. Threads of sunlight struck through, yet its caustic heat was not enough to warm the chill of uncertainty running through her. She reached out her senses to probe the stench. Karma gasped, sucking in a boiling breath, and retreated a little farther away when she saw the shimmering outline of something, someone, just a few feet away.

"You're most welcome," the stranger said, her voice silken as her form filled out. She bowed towards Karma, who did not move an inch. Karma's mouth gaped; her words evaporated before they hit her tongue.

The stranger blew at a fiery heat glowing upon her spectral fingers, tempering their power to a cooler, opalescent hue. She smiled at Karma.

"I felt you could use the help," she said, nodding her head at Karma. "He was particularly nasty and you seem... fatigued."

Taken aback, Karma edged further away, brows furrowed, her mouth snapped closed. Her mind screamed a warning, her fingers curled against her sides... yet she felt a strange bloom within her centre. A warmth, a heat, an almost impossible urge to know this new, shimmering being who appeared to be just like herself.

The stranger inclined her head and held her arms out.

"Well, you seem quite lost for words. I suppose I should make the introductions, then. I am Fate." Fate bowed deeply; inky hair fanned about her upon a breeze that was not there. Her smile widened as she straightened, her complexion shimmered every shade of humanity.

"I apologise if I startled you," Fate said.

That strange, yearning feeling spread within Karma. She could not take her eyes from Fate.

Karma tilted her head, allowed herself to emerge from the ether a little. She moved cautiously forward, entranced by the shape of Fate... enamoured by her very existence. Words took a moment to arrive. Her fingers still curled in and her life force thundered faster.

"You killed him? Why?" Karma asked.

"He was a nasty thing," Fate answered, her smile unwavering, her eyes shimmered like a newly exploded star. "A dark soul, corrupted and foul. He was fated to die this day anyway, so I suppose it was quite good luck."

"I... I was addressing the matter. I assure you I had it thoroughly in hand. Justice was mine to tend, uh, um, Fate," Karma said, trying to hide the annoyance in her tone.

"Indeed, it may well have been your path to choose. Yet," Fate cocked her head, brows quirked and her smile widened. She floated a little closer. Karma stayed her position. If she had needed to breathe, she knew without fail, she would be breathless.

"Dearest friend, I too, felt drawn to fate him, and unlike you, my justice is not a choice. Destiny dictates that my justice is unwavering, unchanging," Fate said, her voice glossy and irresistible. Karma swallowed and edged a little closer.

Fate's smile widened. "I most happily have saved you the effort, perhaps preserved your energy for the next good deed that awaits your most beautiful self." Fate drifted closer again to Karma. Her spectral arms a richer opaque as they rested over where a heart would normally beat. She inclined her head.

"To find kindred after being alone for such a long time, it is now my fate to serve alongside you forever."

"Alone? You too have been alone?" Karma asked, her fingers uncoiling, her form relaxing.

"From the moment the stars birthed me, I believed I existed entirely in solitude. Can you imagine my joy when I heard your song, when I felt your vibration? I have searched for you, for another like myself, for so very long," Fate said.

Karma opened her mouth, but once again, words failed her. She reached a hand out but quickly dropped it by her side.

Am I dreaming? She wondered.

"I am at your unreserved service, dear kindred," Fate's voice was honey, and it wet Karma's mouth.

"May I ask, do you possess a name?" Fate asked.

Karma smiled. Something fluttered deep in her belly. She scoffed at herself, looked to her feet as warmth flooded her face. "Karma, the name whispered to me upon my birth, was Karma." She looked back up, eyes locking more confidently with Fate.

"What do you want of me?" Karma asked. Her energy jittered; nerves flashed through her essence. She glittered like a fading star beneath a blanket of morning sun.

Fate smiled more broadly, filled her presence with colour. Her skin shimmered once more. Every shade of the spectrum, from milk-white to darkest ebony, and every tone in between. Her hair encapsulated the light of the cosmos, darkness pin-pricked with light. It draped down her body, curled around the curve of her hips, hugging them in a way that Karma was now dreaming of. Fate reached for Karma; a slender hand upturned.

"Companionship is what I seek, kindred. Dearest Karma, I have existed for so long, it wasn't until I sensed you, until I felt the reassuring beat of your energy, that I realised how very lonely I was. I knew then that my fate was to find you." Fate's eyes swirled with every colour of the cosmos, bright, wide, inviting.

Karma considered this for a while. Her energy pulsed more rapidly. She quivered a little faster, struck with feelings identical to those she coveted with Kehtut, the same as the passion she had shared with Aka. Loneliness sliced through those warm feelings. A familiar companion that slithered cold within her as she regarded the indescribable beauty of Fate.

Fate was a stranger; an unknown who had interloped on Karma's good work. Despite some strange sense of offense, Karma felt something else twist inside her. A deep warmth pushed the chill of loneliness aside. A fluttering urge raged within her. It made her want to touch Fate, to caress her, to taste and kiss her... to press her ethereal form against her own and sink within her.

The burning sun beat down overhead. It blazed through Karma's essence and bathed Fate in a glorious light. Karma relaxed and bloomed a little brighter. She moved closer to fate and let her form fully emerge from the ether.

"I understand loneliness. It is a most cruel companion. I am grateful to make your acquaintance, Fate." Karma smiled, reached out her now corporeal hand to Fate, and when their fingers laced together, it was as though lightning had struck right through the centre of Karma's existence.

Fate drew her closer. Karma allowed it. She coveted the touch, as though it had always been there to take. Her life force circled and slithered within her. Heat blazed between them. Their energies shimmered with recognition that they were born of the same cosmos, that they were one and the same.

"I have been searching for you for a very long time," Fate whispered. Her eyes roamed Karma's face, gentle fingers cupping her chin.

"And I you. For as long as I can remember, I heard a song, a call, but I could not find the source of that beautiful melody," Karma responded.

"It is now as it was meant to be. Our time has come to pass, and we shall forever more never know the pain of isolation." Fate pulled Karma closer. "Oh, how I have yearned for a companion."

"How did you find me? I searched for so long for you," Karma asked. Every particle of her soul flared, her fingers knitted tight into Fate's, and everything felt so very complete.

"I am Fate, dearest Karma," Fate said, pulling Karma closer and pressing their cheeks together. Karma drank in the crispness of her smell.

"It was fated that we find one another, and it is fate that

I trust," Fate said as she pulled Karma's hand to her lips and pressed them into her palm.

Karma sighed, almost forgetting the passion she shared with Kehtut only hours ago.

"We know the beat of the universe; I feel the very essence of every being, as I know you do too, dear Karma. Together, you and I are destined to reveal life to humanity, to set balance upon it. That is the way it was and always will be. This is all I need to understand. It is all I need to know to do what needs to be done," Fate said.

Karma's mind reeled; she gasped a cosmic sigh that startled birds who nestled on the edge of the nearby roof. The beat of their retreating wings fanned the heat billowing within Karma as she relished the sensation of the touch of Fate's essence against hers. Touch without dipping within the skin of a human was an unexpected bliss. Touch; it was the one feeling she craved so deeply. Touch, proximity... love. And the touch of Fate pushed all sense from her.

Fate leaned in, ran her fingers down Karma's cheek. Karma nodded at her unspoken question, giving permission for that which she desired so deeply. Fate's eyes sparkled, she smiled wider, pearlescent teeth lit her face impossibly brighter, and Fate pressed her lips against Karma's. Karma gasped, just as Kehtut did when Anwar kissed her body in just the right places. Karma's arms dropped to Fate's side. She pulled their bodies closer until their energies ran through each other, melded together...and they burned with passion. That same burning, rhythmic explosion ruptured within Karma. It was that same heavenly release she felt when within Kehtut, at the blissful moment when their love reached its zenith.

"I..." Karma stammered. She pulled away, overcome by the feelings, overwhelmed by bliss.

Fate pulled her close and ran her hands through Karma's hair. She whispered gently in her ear.

"You have been lonely for a very long time. I am here now, my love. No longer shall you yearn. Our energy entwines. We are one and the same. We are everything and nothing." Fate cupped Karma's face, then ran ghostly fingers along her form.

"We *are* love," Fate said as Karma closed her eyes, emotion welled within and diamonds fell down her face. It took all her strength to not flood the entire Earth with her joy.

"I have been so very lonely," Karma whispered.

"Never again will your soul feel empty, for I am Fate and I am here for you, always," Fate cooed and rested her forehead against Karma's. Their lips found each other once more. Karma and Fate melted into each other; their energies entwined as one, and for the first time since time began, Karma did not feel alone. For the first time in an age, she shut out the calls of humanity, closed herself off to pain and fear, and let justice slide away for a moment.

Karma gave all of herself to Fate.

I I

For years, Karma and Fate left the world behind. Loving selflessly, giving of themselves fully to one another. They discovered each other's souls, understood each other's cosmic and terrestrial bodies. Together they melded as one, enduring sun and rain, storm and calm. They blended with flood and drought and cried through the joy and sorrows of life and death.

Their forms moulded perfectly together, each fold of skin, each bend and curvature. The very taste of their essence was incorruptible and perfect. Karma could not unbind herself from Fate. Fate would not release herself from Karma. They revelled in the delight of loving one another.

When the cries of humanity became unbearable, when they could no longer ignore the pain, the suffering and injustice, they unwound their bodies, but did not let each other go. They peered down at the globe that rotated beneath them. Karma and Fate watched and listened, and then they judged.

"I have cared for this world for a very long time," Karma said.

"Of the many worlds across the universes, only this one makes me want to stay, Fate said as her fingers laced a little tighter into Karma's and her energy pulsed brighter. She tipped Karma's face up and looked deep into her eyes.

"I feel a deep calling to remain upon this world. May I stay? May I help you tend to it, sweet Karma?"

Karma pressed her mouth against Fate's. Their tongues smoothed across each other. Karma could barely think. The taste of Fate was insatiable. "Yes, oh my love, yes, please help me in my quest." Karma's voice was a song and their lips joined once more. They plaited their forms together, their passion a nebulous rainbow against the backdrop of space. Their ecstasy peeled across the world through thunder and lightning.

"We shall tend this world together," Karma cried with joy and light bled across the seas.

"So, it shall be." Fate released Karma and rose high into the atmosphere. The moon haloed her beauty, and Karma sighed at the sight. Wind coiled away upon her breath and churned the oceans far below. Fate surveyed the Earth, eyes narrow as they scoured the breadth of it. Her face softened into a smile, and she reached out for Karma, who joined her instantly.

"We will meet each day, dear Karma, where dawn and dusk embrace." Fate pointed to a kiss of light on the horizon. She pulled Karma into her velvet essence. "Between both night and day, we shall love." And love they did. When Karma met Fate, the world tilted on its axis and would never be the same.

12

The sun and moon met along the horizon, aflame in blues, yellows, and orange. Karma and Fate remained a silhouette of passion, a ball of devotion twisting against the backdrop of the Earth. Fate pulled away first. Losing her heat and touch left Karma immediately empty and her light dulled.

"You rush away so early today?" Karma ran her fingers down the softness of Fate's arm, their fingers entwined a moment before they both melted into their cosmic forms.

"Much is to be done today, my love. A long-awaited fate that is most difficult for me," Fate said, turning from Karma, already misting away into the ether.

"Let me help you," Karma called, but Fate was gone, her voice merely an echo, a memory. Karma stared at the empty space left behind where Fate should be. Her eyes pained wide; a void stretched out before her like a black hole ate at her core. She struggled with this vacuous loneliness that flooded in every single day that Fate separated from her. As she drifted away from the equilibrium of night and day,

Karma wondered, more than other days, on what this most arduous task was that Fate spoke of. For so very long they had come and gone, tending the Earth in their own ways, balancing justice, setting the course of humanity into perfect symmetry. Today, however, something felt very different. A gnawing ache deep within her left the world a little unbalanced. Karma's hands returned to nervous balls, rolling and clenching, just as they had so long ago.

As the Earth turned, and the sun became a blinding slice of yellow, Karma drifted higher amongst the clouds where space met the azure cap of the earth.

She pressed against her belly, trying to settle an unease that twisted uncomfortably. An urgent tapping in her mind had her speed along. She whistled for the wind and it picked her up, spurring her through sun and rain, zig-zagging across the light and the dark. Anxiety whipped her into visibility as she descended closer to the ground. The call she heard was unexpected. She changed course, banking south when she had planned to be in the icy tundra of the north.

Karma stared hard at the shapes rushing past below her. The rhythmic flow of coasts, the oceans, the dense verdigris of great forests, and she felt more keenly the many cries for her hand of justice. Her body ached as it always did, her soul in pain for the pain of humanity. Yet, this day, Karma remained troubled by a strange coil of something more that tugged within her. It pulled her back to where the air was rich with spice, where the sun burned the land. Karma trembled as her senses pulled her back to where she had not visited since the time before Fate.

It was a particularly searing summer's day over the same

dusty city in which Karma and Fate had first met. Karma secreted herself within the mists of scattered clouds; hiding, observing the movements below. She was just another white smudge against the cerulean sky, unseen, unheard, but all-seeing.

The city that sliced along the perimeter of the great river had grown. Its palaces and homes exploded near the life-sustaining river bank. The populace had expanded, a great swell of life and death, of justice served and justice forgotten.

Karma felt heavy, there was no smile in her heart. So many thoughts, so many emotions; a cacophony in her mind. What tapped the loudest, though, was the burgeoning pulse of good and evil. It strummed within Karma and relit her senses. It tweaked her attention, and she winced at the enormity of it all.

Karma evaporated into a gust of wind and descended through the crowds. She tapped into men and women, held her breath and felt for their souls. With some, her heart lightened, and she cried with joy, passing them by, leaving them in peace. Shadows stalked others. A thick, syrupy darkness that tasted sour upon her breath. With those humans, Karma billowed with rage and she left her mark upon them. Thousands of faces blended into a million thoughts. Those thoughts more often than not were intentions best left unsaid, along with greed, hunger, and fear. As always, the loudest vibration of all was murder, and this time, the taste of murder held a familiarity.

Karma pulled to a stop and sat within the cool tingle of a cloud. She called out for Fate, overwhelmed by her burden, trying to swallow away the blood she tasted... blood about to be spilled. The ether remained silent. Fate did not respond. Karma stared below the dangle of her feet, at the hustle and bustle of millions. There were just too many.

The sound of humanity was a long, low, guttural cry that underpinned the beat of the Earth. That one voice, however, struck Karma again. A voice that wrapped around her soul and fanned it with warmth. Karma's head snapped left; her mouth fell as she listened intently. The voice cried out louder, a comfort like the first strike of sun upon the horizon. Its tone hooked her, and her body moved towards it intuitively. Karma whispered to the wind again, and it scooped her up, surged into a gust, and drew her along. Urgency fanned through her. The tremble of her form had humans looking her way, squinting their eyes, as though they nearly saw her.

She curved back towards the gentle lapping of the river, oozed through its tall, reedy banks and coursed through the bustling streets towards the oldest part of the city. Karma blew into her wind, coaxing it along. Her breeze lifted her higher and elevated above the noise of everyday mundanity. Sunshine luminesced through her, casting a faint rainbow over the roof line as she turned her ear to the voice calling for mercy.

An icy tear sliced down her face. She gasped, her form stuttered, rigid, almost unwilling to move on, but she forced herself to slip from the wind, fingers clasping by her side. The familiar voice cried again.

"No, no, it cannot be?" Karma flickered, redness momentarily stained her silhouette, and she gained momentum. "Please, wait for me? I am coming," Karma cried to no one but herself. She moved automatically, knowing the way to go without thought, without the need to even see. The heat of the day no longer burned through her, the fire of fear and anger replacing it. The cries of others faded away, as she recognised the voice crying out for mercy.

"Kehtut?" Karma raced faster, reaching the outer edge of the city. The suffocating stench of poverty tainted the air, mingling with the crisp, cool smell of the river. Another voice joined the desperate chorus in Karma's mind. "Anwar?"

Kehtut and Anwar's cries for mercy were distant, fainter by the moment, as though their life forces were being dragged too quickly from them. Karma trembled, disoriented by a strange new feeling... panic. She came to a stop, the wake of her churning the dusty walkways below. Karma reached out into the ether to tap into the couple who had shared with her the joy of love. She called for Fate, but there was still no answer from her beloved.

Karma dove sharply down, her gust toppling a woven basket from the head of a labourer; the commotion startled his donkey to bolt off with its cart. Karma lost control, people screamed wildly as panic tugged her between ethereal and physical form. Humans ran from her, ducked and weaved, cried for the Gods to save them. Flickering in and out of a corporeal state slowed Karma down, and she screamed in frustration. Her roar drew a richer, howling wind that fanned terror amongst the humans.

Kehtut and Anwar's souls were fading, their voices a thin wisp that was almost impossible to hear. Their song of death was nails drawn across stone. It was pain, not the gentle lullaby afforded by a natural death.

Karma fought her way clear, clawing back from her

confused flesh and blood state. She regained the concealment of invisibility. Arriving at Anwar and Kehtut's humble home, Karma found it darkened and deathly quiet. Two infant cradles sat empty; dust settled thickly upon one of them. The hearth glowed dully, untended for a time. Tallow candles were long melted into the window ledge, the odour of the last meal still rich upon the air.

"Anwar? Kehtut?" Karma called, not knowing if they would answer the call of a faceless voice, a ghost, a dream. She searched more frantically, upturning the entire shack. Cobwebs stitched across the small windows; the home felt untended, its energy heavy with sadness.

"Where are they?" Karma's form flickered once more. She thought of Fate, called out to her yet again.

"Love, Love please help me?" Karma pushed back out into the stinking heat of a thin alley that felt as hollow and abandoned as the home she had just upturned.

"Fate? Fate, please?" The dust below Karma bogged with her tears. "Fate, my love, I need you." There was no response.

Where did she say she would be this week? Was it South, was it North? Karma bit her lip, wondering just what it was it that Fate had planned for this day?

Karma elevated into the sharpness of the sun and called on the wind again. Her breeze sped her along, cutting around winding alleys, her ears tuned in solely for Kehtut and Anwar... but they had fallen silent. She breeched a corner, ear cocked. The ether felt thicker, and she couldn't feel her way through it with her normal ease.

Karma's hand slapped across her mouth and her heart pained in a way it never had. Something was hazing her senses, something, or someone was blocking her ability to find Kehtut and Anwar. Sounds dulled, as if she was swimming through sludge. Something she had never felt before pressed her back, an invisible hand, like a door shutting in her face. The reverberation shuddered through her.

Flashing between flesh and phantom, neither here nor there, Karma rushed faster along the river and through the reeds. Her senses were chaotic. All at once she tasted the cool of the water, the minerals of its muddy bed, felt the coarse grasp of its reeds, and the ever-slowing heartbeat of one of the two souls she searched for.

Karma halted as though she had hit another wall. Pulsing like a fading star, her body remained rigid. One of those beloved heartbeats ceased, and she screamed. Birds launched from the trees, they flocked left and right, screeching as storm clouds drew in upon Karma's agony.

At that moment, the barricade released its grip, freeing her from the blockage, and she regained the strength of her senses.

The familiarity of Kehtut's energy still pulsed, but Anwar? She could not sense him at all. Panic pushed her forwards; she rose above the reed bed, their whisper as frantic as the beat of her soul. Searching out towards the middle of the river, where the sun struck across it like glass, she came upon a small, thin boat. It lay upturned, bobbing on the gentle current alongside a length of fabric that curled around the rudder. Within that fabric, the sun hooked its light upon bronze arm rings. A body lapped against the boat.

Thud, thud, thud.

The body had already cooled; its pulsations were gone.

Karma watched from a distance as Anwar's soul pulled itself from his corpse. Its transparent blur shuddered, confused as they always were. It curled upwards and then fell back towards the water. It billowed in and out, garnering strength, understanding its new destiny before it misted away in the heat of the sun. Karma's eyes narrowed, tear-filled and burning.

"No, that's not how it was meant to be!" Karma blinked hard, staring across the water. She gasped silently; her body aquiver once more. Confusion twisted her insides; an ugly beast rose within her as her vision cleared and she saw the truth.

Floating above the corpse of Anwar was Fate.
"My love?" Karma called; an uncertain shake held her voice hostage. Despite every atom urging her to go to Fate, Karma kept her distance. Fate spun around, surprise upon her face, delight in her smile, lust in the glow of her aura.

"My beautiful Karma, what brings you here?"

Karma stared at her beloved, mouth agape, attention sliding between Fate and Anwar's corpse.

"My love?" Fate stretched a hand, her fingers curled inwards. "Come, my love."

Karma's faced darkened, her mouth thinned, and her essence flamed ruby. She did not move.

"Karma?" Fate's smile waned, and her voice lost its honeyed tone.

For a moment, Karma could not find words. The joy emanating from Fate confounded her. A deserving soul had evaporated before his time, before Karma could reward him with the longer mortal life he deserved. This man, Karma had long ago decided, should pass over in the peace of sleep, entwined with his wife, not drown in a river.

"My love, you have not answered me. Why are you here?" Fate's colours faded to a strange, green dullness as she made her way towards Karma.

Karma held up her hand. Fate halted.

"I... I was here to save him, Fate. He was to be given a better destiny than this. He was a good and deserving soul."

"Ahh, I see." Fate's colours shuddered again before they brightened to a pearlescent glow. "We have had a misunderstanding then. It was his destiny to drown. It has passed as it was meant to be," Fate answered without the slightest hint of regret as she watched Anwar's body loosen from the boat, hair fanned like a halo about his bloating face.

Karma held her tears. "That was an awful and unjust death, Fate. It is not what he deserved at all. He had endured a terrible life as a child yet grew into a kind and generous man. I was to reward him, to save him so that when his time came, he would pass in peace," Karma said, her voice thin.

Fate merely arched her brows and shrugged. "It is merely fate, my love. Nothing more, nothing less. Humans know no different."

Anger twisted uncomfortably through Karma's aura and her colour deepened to crimson. She could still sense Kehtut, somewhere close, her heart frantic, her life force in great distress. Karma retreated to the edge of the river where the reeds whispered loudest. She closed herself off to Fate. Her attention fell to frantic splashing below, to Anwar's body, bobbing up and down as the fish began their meal of him. Her eyes slid back to Fate's proud expression and her fingers curled in until the pain caught alight. She had an overwhelming desire to strike out at Fate.

"My dear," Fate reached a hand once more towards Karma and shook her head. Her smile and tone offended Karma as though they were the sourest things she had ever experienced.

"Do not feel unsettled by this. This is my purpose, to seal the fate of these beings, no matter who they are or what they have endured. They are all equal under my watch." Fate moved forwards and offered her yet hand again to Karma. "You, my love, have no hand in this, no guilt to bear."

Karma pulled further away from Fate. The echo of Kehtut's soul tapped urgently in the back of her consciousness. "So, you would kill a good person and let an evil soul live? Do *you* feel guilt for such an atrocity?"

Fate considered the question. She furrowed her brow, looked to the heavens, then nodded. "If that is what I determine their end to be, so it shall be. I have no reservations at all. It is the way of things, my love." Fate glanced over Karma's shoulder, as though she too heard Kehtut's needy soul. Panic raced through Karma.

"That is not right. You cannot reward the bad with happiness and the good with tragedy!" Every particle of Karma ignited with fury. She expanded and coalesced into a just-visible cloud of bloody darkness, an angry smudge against the sky. Her anger stirred the river and its water sloshed heavily at its banks.

Karma spread her arms wide and sucked in the air. The reeds bent in; the wind whistled into her very core.

"Leave my world!" Karma screamed. Lightning sparked from her periphery, setting the reeds ablaze behind Fate. The last of the birds scattered, the river foamed at the shore and churned below her.

Fate recoiled; shock erased her smile.

"Leave? You wish me to leave over a lowly mortal soul?" Fate pressed her hands over her chest, her expression aghast.

"These are *my* mortals, my souls, Fate! I travelled for an eternity to find them, to love and protect them." Karma looked around her, lightning crackling closer to Fate. "This is *my* world, and you have corrupted it!" Karma aimed her power across the roiling river and it forked across the water.

Fate's eyes glimmered red; her shock faded into a thin line of anger. Her hands fell to her sides. "You invited me in, Karma. We are now linked, we are fated to be together, fated to keep this world turning over together... forever." Sparks sizzled behind Fate. Karma fanned the burning reeds into a roar.

Karma's form grew ever bigger, a raging storm of light and dark, of thunder and lightning. A shining light of redemption and forgiveness, ever so momentarily Karma's attention was hooked away, her ear on the soul of Kehtut, screaming louder by the moment.

"That soul is mine too," Fate laughed. "Don't fight me, my love. It is how I have fated it, and it is how it shall be."

Karma flashed luminescent, then her essence disappeared, sucked into the storm she had created. She reached for a lightning strike, surged along its power, and raced towards the hut by the river, towards the cry of Kehtut. Fate was beside her within seconds. They collided over the tallest pyramid, skidded along the desert sands. They tumbled over the dusty city, their energy drew in more clouds, and their lightning ignited a rainstorm that scattered the populace indoors. The city was awash as Karma and Fate twirled and fought in a race for the destiny of Kehtut.

13

Karma's senses were on fire. She peeled away from Fate and skimmed the rooftops towards the fringe of the city. She banked onward to where the fishmongers lived, its smell a beacon as she crested the roof where the screams were fulminant.

Ever aware of Fate behind her, Karma dashed back towards the small home, now rich with the song of terror. She slipped through the tanned flap at the entrance, riding Kehtut's screams. There, upon that same dusty papyrus mat, Kehtut struggled all alone, in labour. She was pale, her skin shone, and sweat beaded into her matted hair. Blood pooled and clotted between her legs. Her knees shook. A babe nestled between Kehtut's thighs, blue and yet to breathe, its cord attached, pulsating slowly as Kehtut's fading life kept the infant alive.

"Please... please let this one live? Gods, please... Anwar, Anwar, where are you?" Kehtut whispered.

Karma fell over both Kehtut and the newborn, draping them protectively. She infused her energy into the infant, urging it to suck in life. Karma then sunk within Kehtut's body, stemmed the bleeding with a breath, and pushed vitality back into them both. All the while, Karma felt the raging heat of Fate circling the ceiling.

"You overstep, Karma. I have not afforded you such an insult!"

Ignoring Fate, Karma untethered herself from Kehtut, watched her revive, then scoop up her babe, and set it to her swollen breast. Karma turned, a protective barrier between Kehtut and Fate.

"She was *mine*, they both were!" Fate's voice was no longer the sweet song that made Karma's soul sing. Her aura was as red as the spilled blood from Kehtut, her energy the complete opposite of Karma's light.

"You will not touch my charges with your dark hand!" Karma said. Her anger shook the small home. Its hearth flickered to life. Kehtut cried out and scuttled backwards, hitting the wall under the small window. Her eyes were wide. "Anwar?"

Karma shadowed her, a veil between life and death. She waved her hand. Kehtut's wide eyes relaxed, her breaths calmed, and she drifted into a deep sleep. The newborn nursed, unaware of anything but its belly filling.

"What have you done to them? Why has she suffered birthing alone? Why has she lost her other child?" Karma's glistening eyes fell momentarily upon the unused, dusty crib. "What did they do to deserve this?" Her light rippled; arcs of energy lashed towards Fate.

Fate curled backwards; she deflected the attack. It hit the roof. Sunlight pierced in through a smouldering hole. "You're going to hurt her yourself if you're not careful!" Fate scoffed, looking down at Kehtut. Karma shielded her further.

"They didn't deserve this!" Karma swept her arm around the home, her finger stopping at the older cradle, the one that should have contained another child.

"*Why* did they deserve it? No one does anything to *deserve* my judgement, Karma. They received no better or worse than anyone else of their ilk. Good or bad, destiny cares not for such things. Now, rest your anger and calm down!" Fate's aura flickered light, then dark, her expression lost all emotion.

"Had I known..." Karma looked down at Kehtut, then back to Fate. "...had I known, I would have stopped you."

Fate smirked, her mouth closed, head shaking. "You have been too busy loving me to notice the world turning. You forgot all about them, Karma. I did not."

Karma gasped. "I...I did not forget them!" The tremor in her voice betrayed the truth.

"I... it doesn't matter if I was distracted for a time. You enraptured me and took advantage of that. I loved you and I thought you loved me, that we loved and trusted one another?"

"And that we do. I love you with my soul, Karma. I am fated to do so, but that does not mean I will relinquish my role in this world."

Karma paled into near invisibility. That strike of sunlight burned through her, straight to the ground.

"I would never betray you..." Karma's voice trailed away, like a leaf on the wind.

Fate's face bunched into a frown. She flicked her hands at Karma.

"Enough now, Karma. I've so much to do beyond this place. Move, my love. It is my right to discharge destiny upon her."

Fate jutted forwards; arms outstretched towards Kehtut. Snoring softly, Kehtut remained unaware of the otherworldliness hovering above her, unaware her fate was not her own to decide.

Karma solidified once more. She blended into a deep shade of purple. Dawn and dusk, love and hate, strength and weakness emanated from her. Karma shimmered, the air about her smudged.

Fate eased back a little, her hands in the air. "Be sensible, Karma. There are millions of these mortals. This is but one."

"Four! One dead husband, one dead baby, and these two will never feel your touch!"

Karma stretched taller; her purple shaded darker until she was almost as dark as the night. Karma's light dimmed, her joy and intrigue dulled, and she realised that her destiny had been forever altered.

"Get out!" Karma screamed. The home quivered again, the ground shook, and she rushed towards Fate. They melted into the walls and fell out into the storm that still raged.

"You are evil!" Karma yelled, her energy arced stronger, truer this time, hitting Fate in her side.

Fate screamed, grabbed her wound. Darkness leaked oily down her side. She retreated, hovering just below the grasp of the storm. Her cosmic hair snapped wildly; her eyes dulled to emotionless ink.

"I am neither good nor evil. I just...am, dearest Karma. Feeling for them is not required. That mistake is yours, and yours alone. You make a grave mistake this day. I am Fate. I was destined to be so, and I shall deliver fate. When I look at people, all I see is their destiny, nothing more, nothing less. I am the great equaliser." Fate pointed sharply towards Karma, her voice deep and ugly.

"You are the one who does injustice, you are the one that causes the scales to imbalance by choosing their destinies rather than allowing fate to impartially balance all life! You complicate simplicity." Fate's smile returned, yet love and lust were a memory in the rage-filled glint of her eyes.

"Then Fate, your scales are broken, and your perceptions are misguided." You... you Fate, are broken." Karma surged towards her, dragging the storm in her wake. Hot barbs pierced through Fate's other side. She reeled backwards; her screech shattered the roofs of a hundred homes. Fate weaved away, a shadow slicing against the rage of the storm, her cries the deepest thunder.

Karma dove deep into the thunder. She plucked out a slice of lightning and chased Fate across the landscape. They circled magnificent temples, criss-crossed the flooding city until they crashed together in the centre of the great river. The river divided, its tide arced up and over the banks. Crops doused; animals drowned. Labourers ran, heads ducked, calling for their Gods to intervene.

Karma and Fate circled each other, both wounded, holding themselves together. Eyes locked, they did not let the other make a move. Day became night, and night lit into day. They watched each other as a hawk circles its prey.

Karma flung out one arm, a sword of light in her hand. She arced it over her head.

"You will submit to me!" Karma's voice was a quake that rocked the earth.

"It seems, Karma, that our fate has changed." Fate cracked her neck, flexed her fingers, and struck a weapon from her hand as well.

"No, Fate. This is not fate. This is karma, and I am yours!"

From that day to this, Karma battles Fate.
Sometimes Karma wins, sometimes she does not.

The End

Thank you for reading, When Karma Met Fate.

If you enjoyed this novella,
please scan my website code below to discover my other
books.

Acknowledgements

As always, many thanks to my family for your unwavering support. You tolerate my constant banter about writing, and I'm quite sure I bore you to tears, but you lovingly listen and encourage me.

To my beta readers, Jas and Jessica. Thank you so much for offering your valuable time to read through my early version and provide feedback. Beta readers are so very essential, and I truly appreciate your kindness and guidance.

To my readers, thank you for your continued support. Writing is an evolutionary journey for me, it is my Karma, and Fate, and I'm honoured to share it with you.

GR Thomas